ZONDER**kidz**

I Can Read!™

BEGINNING READING 1

Princess Petunia's Sweet Apple Pie

story by Karen Poth

This is the Kingdom of Scone.

The grass is always green here.

Dear Parent:
Your child's love of reading starts here!

Every child learns to read in a different way and at his or her own speed. You can help your young reader improve and become more confident by encouraging his or her own interests and abilities. You can also guide your child's spiritual development by reading stories with biblical values and Bible stories, like I Can Read! books published by Zonderkidz. From books your child reads with you to the first books he or she reads alone, there are I Can Read! books for every stage of reading:

SHARED READING
Basic language, word repetition, and whimsical illustrations, ideal for sharing with your emergent reader.

BEGINNING READING
Short sentences, familiar words, and simple concepts for children eager to read on their own.

READING WITH HELP
Engaging stories, longer sentences, and language play for developing readers.

READING ALONE
Complex plots, challenging vocabulary, and high-interest topics for the independent reader.

ADVANCED READING
Short paragraphs, chapters, and exciting themes for the perfect bridge to chapter books.

I Can Read! books have introduced children to the joy of reading since 1957. Featuring award-winning authors and illustrators and a fabulous cast of beloved characters, I Can Read! books set the standard for beginning readers.

A lifetime of discovery begins with the magical words "I Can Read!"

Visit www.icanread.com for information on enriching your child's reading experience.
Visit www.zonderkidz.com for more Zonderkidz I Can Read! titles.

Suppose someone sees a brother or sister in need
and is able to help them. If he doesn't take pity
on them, how can the love of God be in him?
— 1 John 3:17

ZONDERKIDZ

Princesses, Pirates and Cowboys
Copyright© 2012 Big Idea Entertainment, LLC. VEGGIETALES®, character
names, likenesses and other indicia are trademarks of and copyrighted by Big Idea
Entertainment, LLC. All rights reserved.
Illustrations © 2011 by Big Idea Entertainment, LLC.

Requests for information should be addressed to:
Zondervan, 5300 Patterson Ave SE, Grand Rapids, Michigan 49530

ISBN 978-0-310-73282-2 (hardcover)

Princess Petunia's Sweet Apple Pie ISBN 9780310721628 (2011)
Who Wants to be a Pirate? ISBN 9780310721598 (2011)
The Fairest Town in the West ISBN 9780310727293 (2011)

All Scripture quotations unless otherwise noted are taken from the Holy Bible, *New
International Reader's Version*®, *NIrV*®. Copyright © 1995, 1996, 1998 by Biblica, Inc.™
Used by permission of Zondervan. All rights reserved worldwide.

Editor: Mary Hassinger
Art direction: Karen Poth
Cover design: Karen Poth
Interior design: Ron Eddy

Printed in China

12 13 14 15 16 17 /DSC/ 21 20 19 18 17 16 15 14 13 12 11 10 9 8 7 6 5 4 3 2 1

The sky is blue.

And the air smells sweet …

like apples!

This is the Duke of Scone.

And this is Princess Petunia.

Tomorrow is a very big day
in the Kingdom of Scone!
Duke and Petunia are
hosting the Scone County Fair.

Early in the morning,

EVERYONE in Scone

will come to Duke's castle.

There will be great music,

fun games,

and Princess Petunia's

famous lemonade!

There will also be

water-skiing and

donut-tossing.

The day will end with
the King's Pie Contest.
The winner of the contest
will receive the Golden Spatula
and host the fair next year.

So today EVERYONE is baking pies.

Even mean, old Bump in the Knight

is making his famous smash apple pie!

"When I win," he grumbled, "I'll wave my Golden Spatula and CANCEL the Scone County Fair."

Bump didn't like the fair.

He didn't like the noise.

He didn't really like fun!

The other knights were worried.

"We must stop Bump," they said.

"WE have to win the pie contest."

So the knights worked on their pies.

Starry Knight made a shepherd's pie.

Knight Owl made a black forest pie.

Hard Days Knight made a beetle pie.

Yuck!

Then … the knights ran

out of sugar.

"I can't make a beetle pie

without sugar,"

Hard Days Knight complained.

Petunia, Duke, and the knights

went to Bump's castle.

They asked him for some sugar.

"Go away!" Bump yelled.

He threw his pie at Duke.

Hard Days Knight got mad.
He threw his beetle pie
at Bump.
Soon all the knights were
throwing pies!

When the pie fight was over

ALL the pies were ruined.

Bump's castle was a mess.

"Don't come back!"

Bump yelled as the knights

left the castle.

Now the knights had to start over.

They all worked together

at Duke's castle.

Everyone was very tired.

At midnight, someone

knocked at the door.

It was Bump in the Knight.

What could he want?

"May I bake my pie here?"

Bump asked.

"My oven is not working."

"Go away," said all the knights.

BUT Petunia took HER pie

out of the oven.

She put Bump's in.

"God wants us to help each other,"

Petunia said.

"And Bump needs our help."

The next day at the contest,

the king picked two finalists:

Petunia's sweet apple pie

and Bump's smash apple pie.

As the king took his first bite,

he realized Petunia's pie was

not done.

Bump in the Knight won

the pie contest!

The crowd gasped as

Bump raised his Golden Spatula …

and handed it to Petunia

with a piece of smash apple pie!

"Thank you for helping me,"

Bump said with a smile.

That day, the Knights of Scone
taught Bump how to water-ski.

And Bump promised to make

next year's fair the best of all!

Suppose someone sees a brother
or sister in need and is able to help
them. If he doesn't take pity on
them, how can the love of God be
in him? — 1 John 3:17

How you made me is amazing
and wonderful. I praise you for that.
— Psalm 139:14

Who Wants To Be a Pirate?

story by Karen Poth

These are the Pirates

Who Don't Do Anything!

Pirate Larry, Pirate Lunt, and

Pirate Pa Grape are their names.

The three pirates live

on a ship.

Every day they sit

together and do … nothing.

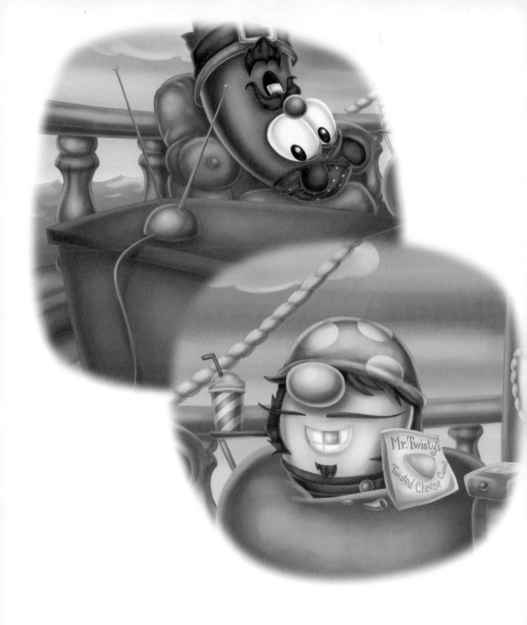

The pirates watch TV.

They wear funny hats.

They eat cheese curls.

They play tic-tac-toe.

And at one o'clock,

the pirates walk their duck.

They always have a lot

of fun doing nothing together.

But one day, Pirate Larry was sad.

"I am tired of doing nothing," Larry said.

"I want to do something exciting!"

"You can't," said Pirate Lunt.

"We are the Pirates

Who Don't Do Anything.

We don't DO anything."

"Then I am tired of being me,"
Larry said.

"I want to be somebody else."

"But God made you," Pa said.

"He loves you the way you are!"

"Come on, guys," Larry said.

"Think about how great

it could be to be somebody else!

Think about how great it

could be to DO something else!"

"I AM tired of tic-tac-toe," Pa said.

"This chalk will never come off my hat."

"Maybe we should move to
TaterTown," Lunt said.
"That would be
an exciting place to be!"

Larry and Pa agreed.

The pirates sat back.

They closed their eyes.

They dreamed of being Taters.

They dreamed of riding

the Tater Train.

They played Tater games.

They wore Tater hats.
They even dreamed of
eating Tater treats!
But …

They didn't like Tater treats.

"Look at these cheese curls!"

Pirate Lunt said.

"They aren't curly!"

Being a Tater was a bad idea.

"We cannot be Taters," Larry said.

"They don't have curly cheese curls."

All three pirates agreed.

Then Larry had an idea.

"Let's go to Cookie Island,"

he said.

"They have great snacks there!"

The pirates smiled.

They closed their eyes.

They dreamed of sailing

to Cookie Island.

It was a long trip.

The pirates got very hungry.

When they arrived, the pirates
roped a giant cookie.
They tugged and pulled.
And pulled and tugged.

They put the cookie on the ship.

The cookie was too heavy!

The ship began to sink!

"I don't want to sail to Cookie Island," Pirate Lunt yelled.

"Too much work," said Pirate Pa.

"Too dangerous," Pirate Larry said.

The pirates woke up from that dream in a hurry!

The pirates thought about it.

The pirates talked about it.

Maybe Larry was wrong.

"It's not so bad being a Pirate
Who Doesn't Do Anything,"
Larry said.

So the pirates ordered
another pizza.
They watched TV.

And at one o'clock, they

walked the duck.

The three friends were

happy just being …

The Pirates Who Don't

Do Anything!

How you made me is amazing and wonderful. I praise you for that. — Psalm 139:14

You will understand what is right and
honest and fair. You will understand
the right way to live.
—Proverbs 2:9

The Fairest Town in the West

story by Karen Poth

Welcome to Dodge Ball City,

the fairest town in the west!

This is Sheriff Bob

and his deputy, Larry.

It is their job to keep the city peaceful

and the Dodge Ball games orderly!

On most days, their job is really fun!

They stop in at the

Rootin' Tootin' Pizza Place.

Then they go see their pals
at the Okie Dokie Corral.

At high noon, Bob and Larry have
a burger at Cow Patty's Cafe.

At two o'clock,

they have target practice

to get ready for the next big game.

They end their day by reading a bedtime
story to the town's one prisoner.
Bob and Larry love their job!

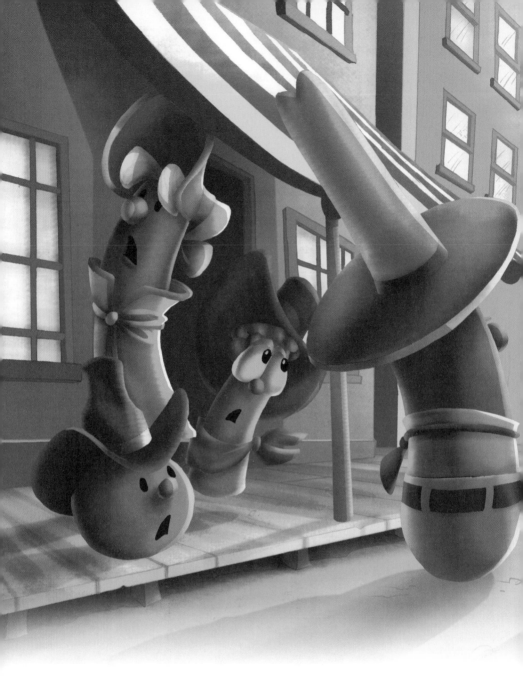

But one day Bob and Larry's job
got a lot harder.

The Ratt Scallion Gang

came to town.

Those Ratt Scallions just
didn't know how to behave!
They said mean things to EVERYONE.

They stole from the people in town.

And worst of all … they cheated!

Soon the whole town was acting this way.

Everyone was cheating.

Everyone was being mean to one another.

Something had to be done!

Dodge Ball City might stop being

the fairest town in the west!

Sheriff Bob got the town together.

He read the rules from the

Cowboy Code of the West.

"Page one," Bob read.

"A cowboy should always treat others
the way he wants to be treated!"

As Bob read the rules,

everyone started to remember

why their town was so special.

They decided
the rules made
a lot of sense!

"Play fair.

Always take turns.

Play by the rules.

"If you cheat all the time,

nobody will play with you!"

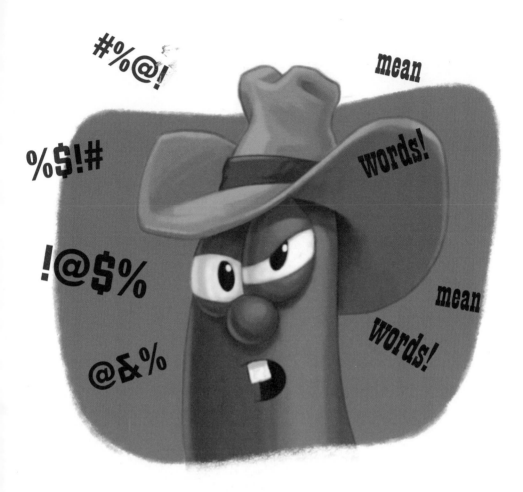

"Use nice words.

"If you say mean words,
nobody will want
to talk to you!"

"Help your neighbor.

"If you're a stinker and don't help your neighbor, Sheriff Bob may put you in jail!"

"So what's it going to be, boys?"

Sheriff Bob asked the Ratt Scallions.

"Can we buy you a root beer, Sheriff?" said one of the Ratt Scallions with a smile.

Bob, Larry, and the Ratt Scallions
went to the Rootin' Tootin' Pizza Place.
They had a lot of fun!

Then they all played a game

of horseshoes … by the rules!

Deputy Larry won fair and square!

Appoint judges and officials for each of
your tribes. Do it in every town the LORD
your God is giving you. They must judge
the people fairly.

—Deuteronomy 16:18